In penguin families when the eggs arrive,
all the mamas go far away to fish. All the dads are
left behind, looking after their egg-babies,
huddled outside in Dad Huddles,
with nothing to eat. Nothing.

Not . . . a . . . thing.

All
the
Way
Home

Debi Gliori

BLOOMSBURY

Little One, if you promise you'll
go to sleep, I'll tell you our story.
It's so secret even your mama
hasn't heard it . . .

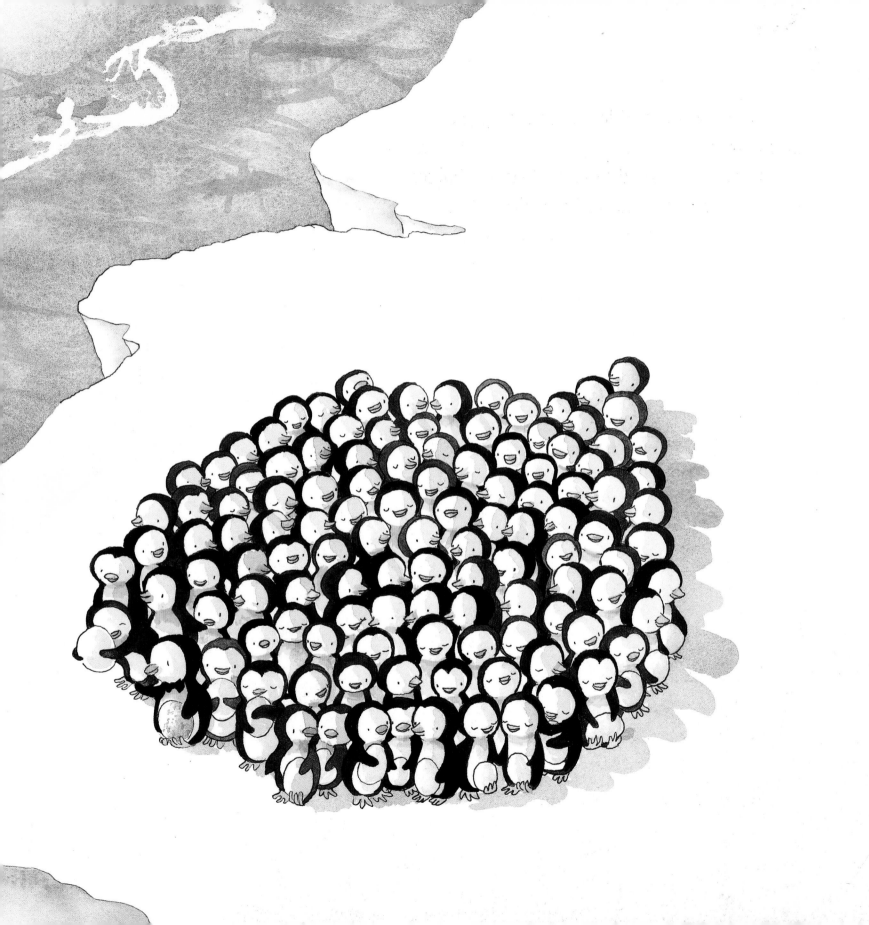

By the time *your* mama had been away
for a week, all I could think about was fish.
I drifted to the edge of the Dad Huddle,
faint with hunger, when . . .

. . . a huge gust of wind
plucked us off the ice and
carried us away. All I could
do was hang on to you. Tight.

The stars streaked past,
the earth spun below until,
at last, the wind dropped.
And we dropped too.

EEEEK!

We fell out of the sky with

a CRUNCH

and a SNAP

and a WHOOOHOO!

Then we crashed to
the ground with a

THUD!

"Never mind," I whispered,
hugging you close.
"Even if we are *lost*, you
aren't hurt and neither am I."

Bravely, I asked a HUGE
Pointy-Eared-Thing where we were.
But it just poked its whiskery nose
into my tummy.

And then . . .

. . . this happened.

Ooops!

Oh dear.
How embarrassing.
Must've been all those fish
I ate last week.

Talking of fish . . .
I could hear water speaking.
It babbled like a river.
And where there's a river
surely there'll be some . . .

YIKES!

Suddenly I wasn't hungry
or brave. Did these pale, pointy
whales eat p-p-penguins?

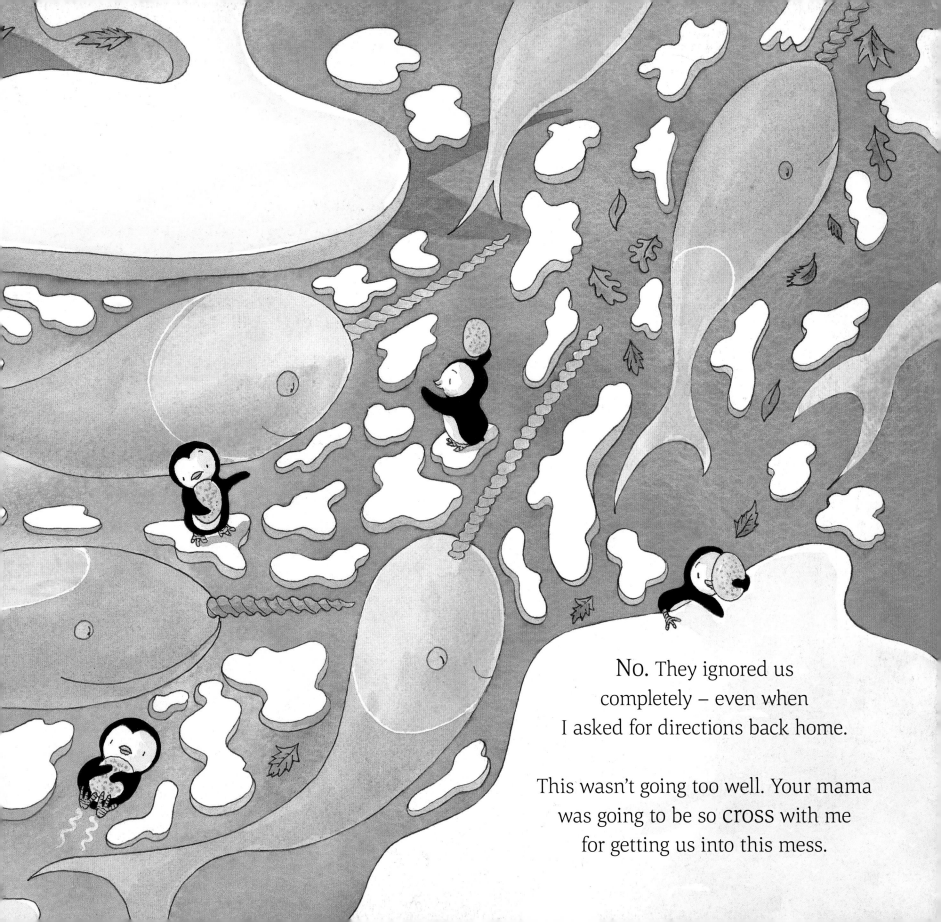

No. They ignored us
completely – even when
I asked for directions back home.

This wasn't going too well. Your mama
was going to be so cross with me
for getting us into this mess.

Somehow I **had** to get back before your mama
returned. I thought perhaps the big
green thing could help us. But . . .

. . . it didn't say much and
it wasn't at **all** helpful.

Why was everything so unfriendly?
Where were we?
How would we ever get all the way home?

I held you close.
I could feel you tap-tapping
inside your shell. The wind
woke up and snow began to fall.

Brrrrrr.

We needed to find shelter
as soon as possible.

Step after step,

we had to keep moving. I tried to
be **brave** but it was so . . . *hard* . . . to . . . keep . . . going.

Just in time, I stumbled into
a hairy, sheltering thing.

It tucked us in between
its wavy ears and carried
us across taiga, tundra,
bogs and ice . . .

. . . until, at last, as light returned to the skies,
we arrived at the most northerly place in the world,
where breakfast was ready and waiting.

Oh, my goodness!
There were herrings
and haddock.
There were sardines
and salmon.

There were mackerel and mullet,
crabs, dabs and sturgeon.

And, just when I was so full,
I felt I might POP . . .

you went POP!

Oh, my!

You were so lovely – so like your mama.
And hugging you and thinking about
your mama and the Dad Huddle
made me so homesick that I didn't
feel brave at all.

Well, talk about lucky!
It turned out that the kindly breakfast chef was also
the Special Air Navigation Transport Authority
and had some parcels to deliver near our home!

He tucked us in to his cart, attached the hairy,
sheltering things and off we went.

Not by land, though. **By air! We FLEW!**
All the way home, back to your mama.

We arrived just in time.
All the mamas were heading
home from their fishing trip.

Quick!

Back to the Dad Huddle.

Mama spotted us immediately.
"What a beautiful baby," she said, adding,
"I've been away for ages. Your poor daddy
must be so hungry and bored by now."

"Oh, no," you said. "We've been far away too.
We went on an adventure! And brave Daddy
flew us home, didn't you, Daddy?"

"Of course," I said. "Penguins are totally brilliant at flying, aren't they, Mama?"

"Flying?" squeaked Mama. "What an imagination. I think you're going to be a brilliant storyteller, just like Daddy."

So, *shhh*, Little One. That's **our** secret.

The True Story of Our Adventure
at the North Pole, and how
we flew there . . . and
all the way home.

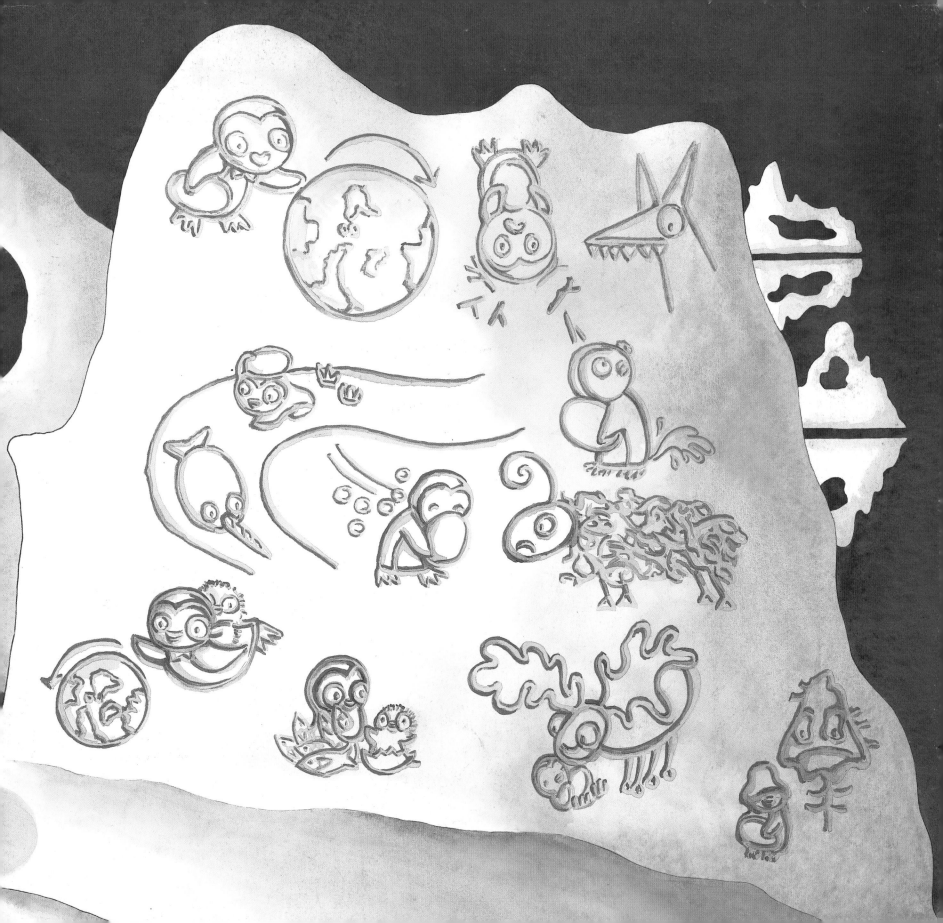

For parents of Very Smalls – this one's for you.

BLOOMSBURY CHILDREN'S BOOKS
Bloomsbury Publishing Plc
50 Bedford Square, London, WC1B 3DP, UK

BLOOMSBURY, BLOOMSBURY CHILDREN'S BOOKS and the Diana logo are trademarks of Bloomsbury Publishing Plc

First published in Great Britain 2017 by Bloomsbury Publishing Plc
This edition published in Great Britain 2018 by Bloomsbury Publishing Plc

A catalogue record for this book is available from the British Library

ISBN: HB: 978 1 4088 7207 9; PB: 978 1 4088 7208 6; eBook: 978 1 4088 7206 2

2 4 6 8 10 9 7 5 3 (HARDBACK)
2 4 6 8 10 9 7 5 3 1 (PAPERBACK)

Printed in China by Leo Paper Products, Heshan, Guangdong

All papers used by Bloomsbury Publishing Plc are natural, recyclable products from
wood grown in well managed forests. The manufacturing processes conform to
the environmental regulations of the country of origin.

To find out more about our authors and books visit www.bloomsbury.com and sign up for our newsletters